Nicki and Niya's First Year

Baby A Meets Baby B

Written by L. Lady Bird Jackson

Illustrations by Kat Glidewell

Nicki and Niya's First Year: Baby A Meets Baby B

Text by L. Lady Bird Jackson

Illustrations by Kat Glidewell

Formatting by Indie Publishing Group

Copyright 2017 LaRonda Ann Jackson

For Nailah Elon and Laiya Elon,

Our double blessings

A window at the Jackson's house flew up with a bang!

Little Breezy stuck out her head and sang to the gang.

"The babies are coming! The babies are coming!"
she shouted with glee.

The guests arriving for the baby shower rushed
inside the house to see.

Big brother Miles carefully guided Mama downstairs.

Cradling her huge belly, Mama eased down into a chair.

"Let's go! Let's go!" Were words echoed from afar.

They came from Daddy who was running
outside to rev up the car.

Vroom! Vroom!

Honk! Honk!

Beep! Beep!

Toot! Toot!

Miles and Breezy put on their coats and
jumped in their boots.

"Stop right there! You cannot go,"
Grandma Pearl said with a stern look.

"The babies will be born in the hospital.
There are no storks in this book."

"Hold on, calm down." Mama pleaded for everyone to remain steady. "The twins are coming early and their room is not ready."

"We will take care of everything,"
was the reassurance Mama heard.

They helped her into the car and threw in her bags
that were sitting on the curb.

Off they raced to the hospital with Daddy
commanding from a distance.

"Bring Miles and Breezy to us later,
after the twins make their grand entrance."

Everyone unwrapping the presents had fun and no trouble.

There were gifts galore and everything was DOUBLED.

Double stockings,

double dresses,

and pink tutus with big swirls.

Double ribbons,

and double bows.

Yes, Baby A and Baby B are girls.

Baby A was born first. She won the relay.

Her cheers of *waa-waa-waa* traveled down the hallway.

Baby B took her time to arrive,
almost an hour in fact.

Her new world was bright and cold,
and there was no way to go back.

"*Waa-waa-waa!*" It sounded like a replay.

The nurse washed and wrapped her
and laid her next to Baby A.

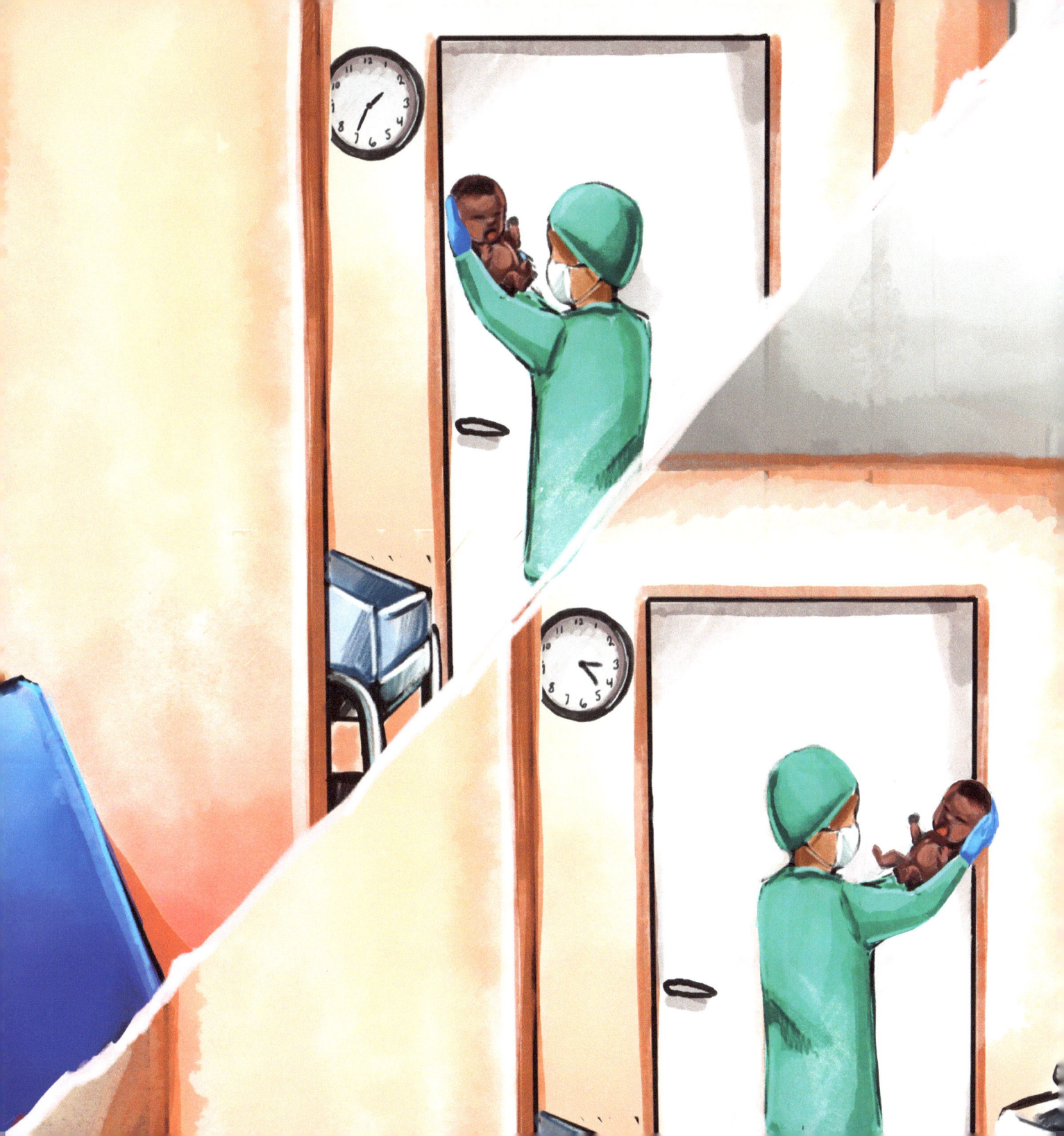

Side by side, and face to face…
such a cute sight to see.

Both new to this world, Baby A meets Baby B.

"No more Baby A or Baby B," Daddy said with insistence.

"It is now Nicki and Niya, names fit for two princesses."

After a few days under the doctor's care,
Mama and babies were as healthy as can be.

"Gather all your children," she said.

"It is now time for this family to leave."

Even with four people helping,
dressing them was not easy.

By the time they were finished,
the twins looked just like Breezy.

Swaddled tightly in their family's arms,
just where they belong…

Two new additions to the Jackson family,

Nicki and Niya…

Welcome home!

L. Lady Bird Jackson grew up in Camden, New Jersey, and graduated from Seton Hall University with a Bachelor of Science degree in nursing.

She lives in New Jersey with her husband and their four children.

For more information, please visit:

labirdhouse.com